BELOW THE
SURFACE

BELOW THE SURFACE

ALLISON FINLEY

ORCA BOOK PUBLISHERS

Published in Canada and the United States in 2023 by Orca Book Publishers.
orcabook.com

Library and Archives Canada Cataloguing in Publication
Title: Below the surface / Allison Finley.
Names: Finley, Allison, author.
Series: Orca currents.
Description: Series statement: Orca currents
Identifiers: Canadiana (print) 20220248842 | Canadiana (ebook) 20220248850 |
ISBN 9781459834538 (softcover) | ISBN 9781459834545 (PDF) |
ISBN 9781459834552 (EPUB)
Classification: LCC PS8611.I653 B45 2023 | DDC jC813/.6—dc23

Library of Congress Control Number: 2022938305

Summary: In this high-interest accessible novel for middle-grade readers, thirteen-year-old Theo finds a pocket watch linked to a local legend about a lost treasure.

Orca Book Publishers is committed to reducing the consumption of
nonrenewable resources in the production of our books. We make
every effort to use materials that support a sustainable future.

Orca Book Publishers gratefully acknowledges the support for its publishing
programs provided by the following agencies: the Government of Canada,
the Canada Council for the Arts and the Province of British Columbia
through the BC Arts Council and the Book Publishing Tax Credit.

Edited by Tanya Trafford
Design by Ella Collier
Cover artwork by Getty Images/Image Source and
Getty Images/Joseph Morgan / EyeEm
Author photo by Ara Arbabzadeh

Printed and bound in Canada.

26 25 24 23 • 1 2 3 4

For Kathy and Glenn,

treasure hunters and explorers.

Chapter One

Something bad happened in my town a long time ago.

I don't believe in ghosts, but my best friend, Syd, swears that last September she spotted the one said to haunt Sawyer's Bridge. She was walking home after dark when she saw a figure in a long coat crossing the bridge toward her.

When the man got halfway across, Syd blinked and he was gone. Lots of people have seen him over the years, but no one can agree on why he's on that bridge or what he's waiting for.

The way I see it, if there *is* a ghost, we have something in common. We both haunt the bridge. There's no need to get in each other's way. He can have the night, and I'll take the day.

Now that summer break has started, I'm out here almost every day, searching for treasure. There's a boat-rental place upriver where people launch rafts and kayaks. Thing is, they aren't too careful and tend to drop sunglasses and phones and even wedding rings into the water.

I find them in the silt and do my best to return them to their owners. Phones are easiest, as long as they still turn on. And for anything I can't identify, Syd's dad is always happy to help. He runs the local pawnshop and keeps a lost-and-found box for all the stuff I bring in.

Today, though, there aren't any phones. The almost-noon sun bakes my bare shoulders, but it feels nice after the cold river. The empty cans and fishing lures are laid out on the wooden planks of the bridge. It's the least impressive photo shoot ever. There isn't even a cool lure in the bunch, just plain weights and hooks. But I log everything, even the boring stuff, on my social feed.

There are a bunch of us who look for lost things, but the serious ones are looking for *old* stuff. They take their metal detectors through fields, searching for history. Sometimes they go places where important things happened a hundred or more years ago. I'd like to try that someday, but I like my river. It's familiar. It comes from the mountains and flows out to the sea. For this brief stretch under the bridge, all the possibilities it carries are mine…if I can catch them.

Except there hasn't been anything interesting for a while. I'm starting to feel a little lost myself.

Just as I'm taking the first picture of my finds, I hear something that freezes the water on my skin.

A horrible laugh carries over the rush of the river.

Oh no.

My heart kicks into high gear. I sweep the cans and lures into my mesh bag, along with my phone in its waterproof case, and jump feet first into the river. My swimming goggles flap around my neck. It's only fifteen feet to the water. I dive from the highest board at the pool, no problem. But the pool is deeper.

The water catches me, bouncing me up and down, and it takes me a second to find my place in the current. I kick to the surface and break into the air with barely a gasp. A dozen bike tires rumble over the uneven boards of the bridge. The boys on the bikes are still cackling like hyenas, but they don't notice me. Only one of them glances at the puddle the cans and I left on the wood. He doesn't look further.

They don't see me this time.

I lie back, my toes catching the breeze above the surface, and let the river carry me away. My heart is still pounding at the near miss, and I need a moment to breathe. My mom says I'm "conflict averse." She doesn't say it like it's a bad thing, but it doesn't feel good. I don't like arguments or fights or any kind of confrontation. They make my heart beat fast when I'm standing still, and I can't think straight.

What can I say? I'd rather go with the flow.

I manage to get my goggles back on without too much water inside them. I flip over to scan the riverbed drifting by under me. Among stones and tangling river plants, a half-crumpled can catches the sunlight. When I dive down and pluck it, a cloud of silt puffs up. I'm already moving on as I shove the can into my bag.

Hold on. One of those stones didn't look right.

I twist around and grab a big rock to help me push against the current. I shove my hand into the cloud of silt and—*there*! I grab something way too smooth and light to be a stone. It's round and flat and fits in my palm.

The air is starting to burn in my lungs, and my mouth wants to fly open. I shove the weird object into my bag and kick for the surface.

The current carries me a little farther as I swim for the riverbank.

A guy fishing on the bank waves. "Nice day to be on the river, eh?"

"Always. Hey, want some weights?" I grab the handful of lead weights tangled in fishing line out of my bag.

"These are in good shape. Thanks." He touches the brim of his hat, which has brightly colored lures stuck into it.

"Have a good one!" With a wave goodbye, I climb the bank, using bushes to haul myself up. The path that follows the river is mostly empty. As I head back toward the bridge, water sloshes from my swim shorts and shoes. There's a trail of dark gravel behind me. It looks like a river monster decided to go for a walk.

I dig into my mesh bag for the mystery item. Out of the water, it's *very* cold. I pull it out and am surprised to see a watch. It looks like the pocket watches old-timey people on TV have. My mom's obsessed with those shows.

One side has a design etched into the metal, and the other side is plain. There's a button on the top, but it won't budge. There must be silt stuck in it. No matter how hard I push or pull, I can't get it open.

"Theo!"

My body jerks in surprise, and I drop the watch.

Chapter Two

The watch bounces toward the bushes and the steep incline, but I grab it before it can disappear. Clutching the watch to my chest, I turn to face the person who shouted.

Thankfully, it's *not* my mom yelling at me for going swimming in the river alone. It's just Syd. Her wild blond hair and freckles stand out in the summer sun. She's wearing a faded-black band

T-shirt and jeans cut off at the knees. Four years ago she decided we were going to be best friends. Who was I to argue with that? I hope she never changes her mind.

"Want some lunch?" She lifts a paper bag, and I see the logo for the local café on the side. My stomach rumbles loudly. I guess swimming and climbing for two hours works up an appetite.

Syd drops onto a bench while I run to get my backpack. I keep it stashed in the bushes under the bridge while I'm in the river. It's got my shirt, water bottle, sunscreen and house key.

As I sit down next to Syd, she hands me a fresh sandwich wrapped in wax paper. I barely manage to say, "Thanks!" before I sink my teeth into it, and mustard and mayo splurt everywhere. The Creekside Café seriously has the best sandwiches in town.

"Find anything good?" Syd asks as she unwraps her own sandwich.

I'm still chewing a massive bite, so I hold out the watch without a word.

Syd's eyebrows shoot up. "That's new. I mean, it's really old, but you know what I mean." She forgets her lunch and takes the watch. She tilts the etched side in the sun and squints. "Is that a ship? This thing needs a polish."

When the button won't budge for her either, she pulls a Swiss Army knife from her pocket. The watch doesn't stand a chance against Syd. She's got the thin blade in the crack and—*click*. The clasp releases and the lid opens a fraction.

"You did it!"

"It's all about how you twist your wrist." Syd grins as she hands the watch back.

The hinge is stiff, and I'm afraid of breaking it, but I've got to see what's inside. I gently pry it open to reveal the watch face. The numbers are all fancy and loopy, and there are words in cursive under the twelve. The hands are stuck at ten forty-six.

"What's that?" Syd says, pointing to the inside of the lid.

Someone's written something right into the metal, but it's hard to read. Some of the shapes don't even look like real letters.

Syd rubs her thumb over it and slowly reads, "*Son...fearless...ports...you*? It's too hard to read like this." She flips it over and frowns. "What does this look like to you?"

Next to her finger are small, precise scratches that look a lot like letters. "What's J.R.?" I ask.

"Not what, who!" Syd's eyes are bright with excitement. "If you find out, you can return it to them."

I scoff. "There's no way whoever lost this is still walking around town. It's been down there for ages." I *wish* I could return it. How epic would that be? Something like this was sure to be missed. I could've put a big wrongness to right. At least I have something other than cans and lead weights for my feed though. This is by far the coolest thing I've ever found.

Syd closes the watch most of the way but not far enough for the clasp to catch again. I snap a photo of it in her palm to post straight to my feed.

I chew on my lip as I hesitate over the caption. With a snicker, I type *Anybody lose this?*

The joke feels a little hollow. I know no one will answer, but I wish they would.

Chapter Three

The mower's electric engine stutters and dies. I fall over the handle with a groan. I only have five feet of grass left to go! Maybe Mom won't notice before I get the battery recharged.

When I got home from the river, I found a note on the counter. Mom's working late again—big surprise. She's got a huge project at work with a deadline coming up. I've barely seen her in weeks.

I don't mind though. She's promised an adventure once the project is done. Maybe we'll get to go to the lake an hour away.

The note said dinner was in the fridge...but it also had a list of chores.

Chores around the house are the one thing she expects from me. In return, she trusts me to do whatever I want during the summer, as long as I stay out of trouble. It's a pretty great setup. But I have a *mountain* of chores this week.

Since Mom's work deadline turned into crunch time, the backyard has become a jungle from neglect. Apparently she's being nice by only making me mow the lawn. Her words, not mine. The truth is, I'm relieved. I don't know what she'd do if I pruned any of her prize plants the wrong way, and I don't want to find out. Mom calls the backyard her "oasis from the madness." She actually enjoys gardening, pruning and getting generally covered in dirt.

I'm not complaining. Since she relandscaped the yard a few years ago, she doesn't ground me as much. Instead of "the perennial morons at the office," she gets a dreamy look on her face over "perennial native flowers."

My phone makes a quiet *ping* in my back pocket. When I fish it out, I reread the number of notifications three times and still don't believe it. I couldn't hear my phone over the mower. It looks like the watch is popular.

My usual number of likes on a post is under ten, with one or two comments at most. The watch has over twenty comments already, and they keep coming. Most of them are variations on *wow!* and *so neat!* and other obvious things.

One of my followers, dane_stone77, wrote, *Great find! Is that a 1905 Nomos?* and tagged a user called Clockwork_Carl. *That's* never happened before.

A light, tingly feeling starts in my toes and crackles to the top of my head. Dane_stone77, vice president of the local metal-detecting club, took notice of *me*. He always posts the coolest things.

Guess I've finally found something the *serious* treasure hunters are into.

And sure, finding old stuff is neat, but you can't give it back to anyone. The person who dropped a coin in 1892 isn't looking for it anymore. But those folks who spent all day rafting and can't find their phone or ring? That's something I can make right.

This pocket watch doesn't exactly have a contact list I can call to figure out who J.R. is. There have probably been hundreds of J.R.'s who've lived here over the years. Syd said I could return it to whoever dropped it, but there's just no way. It's too old, and I don't have any decent clues to go on.

But I don't like giving up. Dane_stone77 and Clockwork_Carl want to know the make of the watch. I want to know who dropped it, even if I can't return it to them. Otherwise it's incomplete. An open-ended mystery.

I've got to know the truth and close the loop.

I'm not alone either. Among the *wow* and *cool* comments, a few people have made wild guesses at who might have dropped it. A lord on a horse, or a young lady fleeing an engagement in the middle of the night.

No way. They've been watching the same shows as my mom.

But one comment isn't like the rest. A fist squeezes the air out of my lungs, and my fingers holding the phone feel numb. It's a short comment, but it gets the point across. *That's not yours. Give it back or else.*

I'm too frozen to move. But under the cold, gripping fear is a thought. Someone knows who J.R. is. And they don't want *me* to know.

Chapter Four

I barely slept last night.

I left the watch and my phone on the kitchen table. I imagined that whoever had left the comment would reach through the screen and grab me. It feels silly now that the sun is up, but it didn't last night in the empty house before Mom got home. Both the watch and my phone are heavy in my pocket for the whole walk to Main Street.

The bell over the pawnshop's door jingles as I step inside.

The bored girl behind the counter doesn't look up from her comic book. It's my sacred duty to entertain her while she minds the store for her dad, and I don't take the responsibility lightly.

"Hey, Syd."

Syd straightens up in an instant. She goes from zero to sixty in the blink of an eye. "Theo! What's up? Find out anything cool? Sorry I couldn't stay out long yesterday. I'm still working off my debt." She lifts one cover of the comic book to show me the latest issue of *Pirates from Galaxy Zero*.

"Didn't you see the comments on my post?"

She rolls her eyes at my question. "News flash— I still don't have a fancy phone." Oh, I forgot. Her parents only let her have a flip phone so they can track her down when they need to. But I know Syd well enough to know it isn't much of an excuse. Even if she had a smartphone, it wouldn't pull her away from her comics.

"Did you bring it?" she asks.

It's my turn to scoff at a silly question. Full of swagger, I put the pocket watch on the counter.

Syd takes one look at it and *tsks*, like the state of the watch is a personal insult. I hold back from teasing her as she retrieves a bottle of cleaner and a cloth from under the counter. While she wipes and polishes, I wander through the pawnshop.

Guitars and other instruments hang on the wall. Piles of jewelry and knick-knacks fill the glass cases. All sorts of old things crowd the tops of the cases. Two porcelain dolls that are definitely haunted sit next to a pile of musty old hats.

No wonder Syd didn't have as big a reaction to the watch as I'd hoped. She sees stranger stuff all the time. But only the box on the shelf behind her has things that came out of the river. Her dad's bold letters spell out *Lost and Found*.

Inside are all the things lost in the river that I couldn't return to their owners. Things like phones that wouldn't turn on, sunglasses and a couple of hats. There are even bracelets, wristwatches and rings. If they're still unclaimed after a year, Mr. Sterling lets me decide what to do with them. Some I keep or give to my friends, and Mr. Sterling sells the rest. He gives what we make to local charities, even though Syd would rather take the money straight to the bookstore to buy more comics.

Syd puts down the cloth. "That's as good as it's gonna get."

I hurry back and can see the difference right away. Instead of the dull, blotchy surface, the watch shines under the lights. The full inscription inside is readable now. *Son, sail fearlessly for unknown ports. We are with you always. March 7, 1962.* The date barely sinks in. I'm too caught up in the words. Sail fearlessly? I wish I could.

"Check it out." Syd points under the initials on the back, where her cleaning has revealed some faint numbers. They're shallow and hard to read, and they don't match the letters on the inside. They must have been carved by hand.

"1967?"

"Know what happened around then? The bridge ghost died. I mean, the *person* died and became a ghost." Syd looks as matter-of-fact as if she's telling me it'll rain on the weekend. "You'd better give it back, or he'll be mad."

My lips purse skeptically. "I don't believe in ghosts." They're as made-up as unicorns. Besides, only one person has demanded I give back the watch. I don't think a ghost from the 1960s knows how to use social media.

"Suit yourself." Syd picks up her comic book and goes back to reading. Conversation over. She may as well be saying that if I get haunted, it's my own fault.

I suppress a groan. "Okay, fine. What can you tell me about the bridge ghost?" It takes a lot of effort to not make air quotes around *bridge ghost*.

Syd's eyes flick to me over the top of her comic book. I try to look as sincere as I can. It must work, because she sets down her comic again. "A penniless traveler arrived in town, hoping to catch the next train. The train was delayed, so he had to stay for a week. But then he died."

"That's it? He just up and died?"

"I didn't come up with it. That's the story Danny told me. His version had more flair."

Danny, who's in our class, has four older siblings, so he learned all the town's weird stories before the rest of us. Doesn't matter if he tells them around a campfire or a tilted-up flashlight—he *always* has an audience.

I have more questions than answers, but Syd did give me a lead. I doubt this watch belonged to anyone as interesting as the traveler in the story. More likely I'll match the initials to a half dozen locals in the old town records. I might find out their job and who lived with them, but anything more than that will be a miracle.

But no matter who the watch belonged to, they were a real person at some point. Real people leave clues. I've got to at least try to find the true story behind this watch. Whoever it belonged to had big dreams and courage, according to the inscription.

I've got to find out why their watch ended up in the river.

Chapter Five

The pawnshop's door falls shut as I step outside.

A cool breeze takes the edge off the sunny summer day. I head down Main Street toward the local museum. As I pass the Creekside Café, I slow down to peer past my reflection in the glass. Looks busy. I'd like a lemonade, but I want to solve this mystery more. With a shrug, I keep walking.

I haven't gone fifteen feet before I have to stop anyway to wait for the traffic lights to change. I roll back on my heels, hands in my pockets, and watch the clouds drift by.

Voices carry from down the block, and I glance to my left. Like a lightning strike, my chill mood is replaced by pure adrenaline. I jump behind the edge of the building, out of sight of the boys down the block, and press my back to the sun-warmed bricks. Two of the boys on bikes were waving to a third coming up the street.

My heart thuds against my rib cage. I don't think they saw me. If they had, they would have shouted. If they had, they'd be pedaling this way to make my life miserable just for the fun of it.

My eyes dart from the *don't walk* hand to the traffic lights for the opposite direction. *C'mon, change!* The green light turns to yellow, then red. A second later the crosswalk signal switches to the little man. I'm like a sprinter off the mark, dashing across the street. I barely glance both ways to make sure no one's ignoring the signal.

Once I'm across the street and there's half a block between me and the boys from school, I slow from a sprint to a light jog. Thankfully it doesn't look like anyone's following me.

That was too close.

I let out a shaky breath. I'm not going to let them ruin today for me. With every step, I put them farther behind me.

By the time I reach the front door of the museum, my good mood is back. This is one of my favorite places to visit. It used to be a house years ago, and it isn't hard to imagine a family from the 1920s living here. I bet there are loads of secrets in the walls, but I don't think the curator would like me prying up boards to find them. She's nice though. Whenever something I find is too old or weird for Syd's dad to figure out, I bring it to Ms. Vardanyan.

The front door creaks when I push it open. The air inside is still and stuffy, and dust motes drift in the beam of sunlight coming through the front windows. It's dead quiet inside, just how I like it. When schools or Scout groups visit, the museum fills with noise, and it's hard to concentrate.

Ms. Vardanyan looks up from behind the front desk and smiles. "Good morning, Theo! What brings you in today?"

"Can you help me with this?" I hold the pocket watch out to her.

Her mouth makes a small O, and her eyebrows shoot right over the top of her glasses. She takes the watch so gently it could've been made of dandelion seeds. "You found this in the river?"

I grin, filling with pride. "Sure did." I don't know why, but I feel like swinging for the fences. I've got to rule out the wildest possibility before resigning myself to town records and farmers. "Syd thinks it could be connected to—" Would she laugh if I said *bridge ghost*? "The, uh, traveler…who died…"

I must've given something away, because she looks at me exactly how I looked at Syd less than ten minutes ago. My cheeks warm, and I hope she thinks I'm sunburned, not blushing.

"Ah, you mean everyone's favorite ghost?" Ms. Vardanyan pries open the lid, turns the watch around and examines it a lot more closely than I did. But I guess she knows what she's looking for. "He's more than just an urban legend. I wish more folks were interested in facts."

"I am!" I say it too quickly, but her laugh isn't mean. I never thought about who the traveler was other than someone passing through town who, well, passed away. Then he started hanging out at the bridge, same as me. Only seems natural. It's where I go when I'm feeling lost and not sure where to be found.

"Okay then, detective, I think I can help you." Ms. Vardanyan snaps the watch shut and offers it back to me. Something in her eyes and the arch of her brow makes this feel big. Important. If I take the watch back instead of leaving it with her at the museum, I'm committing to the cause.

I don't even hesitate. The weight of the watch feels *right* in my palm. There's a connection between me and whoever lost it.

"This way." Ms. Vardanyan leads me through the room showcasing early colonial history. There are displays about the people who came to explore, to search for gold and to build farms. The next room is dedicated to the Indigenous people who have cared for the land since way back and still do. It used to be a sitting room and has a big window looking out onto a yard full of wildflowers.

Next is modern history, but by *modern* they mean the last hundred years or so. Can it really be called that if it happened before television existed?

Ms. Vardanyan leads me to a tall glass case against the back wall. The sign above it reads *Local Lore*. The shelves, crowded with framed papers and photos, and other random things, looms over me.

There are sections about Bigfoot sightings and the sea monster that lives in the nearby lake. *They* didn't lose a pocket watch.

There are things about people too. A gang of rum runners from the 1920s grabs my attention before Ms. Vardanyan points to the bottom left corner.

"Most of what we have about the traveler is there. Sit tight and I'll get the rest."

I don't know why, but the small assortment of items and papers makes me sad. This is all that's left of someone whose big dreams carried them far from home. I sit cross-legged in front of the display for a better view.

There isn't much. A room receipt for an inn. A train ticket. A few coins that aren't Canadian. Despite sharing a bridge with an urban legend,

I don't know anything about the real person who inspired it. I wonder where he came from and where he was going.

Could this watch belong to him? How could a pocket watch wait in a river for over fifty years, not far from where it fell? Unless a ghost was watching over it until just the right moment.

No way. There's no such thing.

I refocus on the display and the *real* clues. There's a framed newspaper article with the headline *LODGER AT INN FOUND DEAD*. The letters are small, and there isn't much to the article. It must have been tucked in a corner of one of the inside pages. I scan the text, but there isn't anything concrete to go on. The innkeeper's daughter found him dead in the armchair by the fire. The sheriff guessed his age to be around twenty-five. Two local men claimed to have found the traveler stumbling down the street and helped him back to the inn. That's it.

The room receipt is yellowed with age and a bit crumpled. The handwriting is hard to read, but on the signature line...I lean so far forward that my breath fogs the glass. The name is impossible to read, but the initials stand out clearly. J.R.

I hold up the watch to compare them side by side.

They're common initials, but...it's gotta be a match. Unless it's a coincidence and the universe is laughing its butt off at me right now. Still, it feels like the watch should be on the other side of the glass with the rest of the things the traveler touched. I want to believe it's his. So how did it end up in the river?

"Theo?"

I nearly jump out of my skin, but see it's only Ms. Vardanyan coming back. She's flipping through some papers and doesn't notice how she startled me. I try not to look like my heart is running a marathon in my chest.

"Here are all the documents that mention the traveler. I hope they help."

The paper on top is a photocopy of the framed article from 1967. They're probably mostly newspaper clippings, and I've already seen how detailed *those* are. They're something to look at if I get stuck anyway.

"Thanks." I glance back at the display, and an idea hits me. The name of the inn is very familiar. Pretty sure there's an old wooden sign with it on Main Street. "Are the Thistledown Inn and Thistledown Books related?"

"Sure are. Mrs. Sorensen's son converted it to a bookstore a few years ago, after she died."

My mind is already racing out the door and down the street to the bookstore, but I stop halfway to the door. I whip out my phone to post a photo of the display to my feed—a good detective always documents their clues. But just before I hit the Post button, my burst of excitement fizzles. If I post this, whoever left the "or else" threat will see it. Clearly they want the traveler to fade away and be forgotten.

I can't let that happen. I tap the button. The traveler may not have left behind many physical objects, but he had a life and he deserves to be remembered.

While the photo is still uploading, I call the pawnshop.

Syd answers on the second ring, in a bored voice. "Sterling Pawn and Antiques, how can I help you?"

"Hey, Syd, it's me. Meet me at the bookstore?"

I'm only asking her to hang out. It's not because she's better than a bodyguard. Honest.

Chapter Six

I hurry up the street and see Syd leaning against the brick wall outside the bookstore. Her hands are shoved in her pockets, and she's watching the cars go by.

"Hey, Syd!"

She grins, a single dimple appearing in her cheek. "I've got a couple hours before I have to be back. Let's make this good."

As we step inside, I'm hit with the smell of old books and wood. One half of the store is for used books, the other for new ones, and there's a spinning rack of comic books between them. I know for a fact Syd was here yesterday, yet she can't help but give the rack a once-over.

At the sound of the bell over the door, the owner, Mr. Sorensen, pokes his head around a bookshelf in the back. "Welcome! Let me know if you need anything."

I lift my finger, about to speak, but he's already gone back to shelving books. I shrug my shoulders to Syd in a silent question. She lifts her eyebrows, full of meaning, and tilts her head toward the back corner, silently saying, *Go on!* So much for backup.

As I make my way toward the looming shelves, I glance back to make sure Syd's coming with me. She's not. She's searching through the comics display. The rush of annoyance overrides my nerves, and I charge ahead.

My bravery fades in the five steps it takes to reach Mr. Sorensen. "Um. I was wondering..."

He pauses his work. He has a faint smile that doesn't quite reach his eyes.

I clear my throat and push out my words. "Do you know about a traveler who stayed here about sixty years ago? He died?" It's so vague—there's no way he'll know what I'm talking about. I'd rather walk out the door than say *bridge ghost* again.

Before I can apologize for bothering him, he says, "What about him?" Mr. Sorensen's smile is gone, and all his attention is on me. This feels like another test. If this is where J.R. stayed, Mr. Sorensen must've been asked about him loads of times. And not always for the best reasons.

"I want to find the truth. Do you know what happened to him?"

I must have said the right thing, because Mr. Sorensen relaxes back into being friendly.

"My mother's the one who found him." He gestures to the room on the other side of the shop, past Syd and the comics. "Right over there. She was bringing him tea, because he'd been out late and his boots and pants were soaked through."

A chill works its way up my spine. He was here more than fifty years ago. Right here.

"They all assumed he had an unknown health problem. It was 1967—they didn't dig into every mystery. There was barely enough money on him to settle the bill. The sheriff must not have thought the death was suspicious, because he didn't ask for an autopsy. Still, it's a shame not to know…" Mr. Sorensen trails off with a shrug.

Hearing all the holes in the story is so frustrating. Can't anyone else see them? A health problem doesn't explain how the watch ended up in the river. If J.R. didn't have much money, he wouldn't have thrown it away.

I take the watch out of my pocket. "Would your grandfather have taken this as payment for the room?"

Mr. Sorensen blinks at the watch in surprise. "Sure. He collected quite a few trinkets from the folks who came through town."

I show him the inscription. "Does this mean anything to you?"

He reads it a few times, frowning. "*Unknown ports*. That's odd. It *is* familiar." He straightens abruptly and snaps his fingers. "Wait a moment! I might have something for you."

Mr. Sorensen disappears through the door behind the counter. After a minute of scuffing my feet on the old carpet, I wander over to Syd. She's deep into a comic, and I know better than to interrupt.

From here I have a better view of the fireplace. Without meaning to, I drift toward it. The wooden mantel is carved with vines and flowers, full of nooks where a latch might be hidden. If I find the right one, a panel might pop open—

"Got 'em! That quote is in here."

I jerk away from the mantel as though it burned my fingers. Mr. Sorensen's at the counter with a small bundle of papers. I hurry over to him.

Upon a closer look I see they're old letters tied with a ribbon. The one on top is addressed to *J. Reid, care of O'Malley's Inn, Maple Hill Ave, Halifax.* Another J.R.! This makes a clear link between the young man who stayed at the inn and the owner of the watch. Syd's gut instinct was right after all. And now, thanks to the clue at the museum, we have our next lead. There's got to be answers in this stack of letters.

"I found these when I was cleaning out the attic last year. Once I realized none of the names in there belonged to my family, I set them aside. The attic is full of things people left behind over the years." Mr. Sorensen slides them across the counter to me. "If you can find who they belong to, you'd be doing me a big favor."

"I will!"

"One more thing. There's an old grave in the cemetery with this name on it. My mother always insisted on leaving flowers there. I never asked why." Sadness settles over him at the thought of a lost secret. "You should check it out. Good luck."

I gulp. A grave?!

Chapter Seven

There are two cemeteries in town. One is flat and often mowed, with headstones sunk into the soil. It has plenty of space. The other is old and overgrown, tucked beside the old church. The windows are boarded with wood, and a rusty chain keeps the doors shut. Dry leaves huddle in the corners of the front step, and the grass has grown long and scraggly at the base of the walls.

My face is locked in a grimace, and I can't take my eyes off it. It's the middle of a sunny day, but still. It's creepy. One kid in my class claims he heard wailing coming from inside the church on Halloween. But I don't believe in ghosts. It was probably just some kids pulling a prank.

Syd nudges my shoulder. "C'mon. Mr. Sorensen said the gravestone is on the northwest side, under a tree."

"How do *you* know which side is the northwest?"

"Because, unlike you, I have a sense of direction." Syd is already striding around the corner. I follow doubtfully.

I trust Syd, but I can't help checking all the gravestones I pass. They're tilted and broken and covered in moss. Rain and time have worn the letters down so they're hard to read. Names, dates and messages of love begin to blur together as I slowly make my way from stone to stone.

"Here! I found him!"

My head jerks up at Syd's shout. She's standing under a big oak tree, facing a simple headstone. With the sun shining through the leaves at an angle, it looks too cool not to take a quick photo for my feed. I don't bother to caption it and hit *post* while I'm already running.

Syd kneels before the headstone and brushes away moss and dirt. There isn't much to read.

J. Reid. April 7, 1967. A journey cut short.

A shiver ripples over my skin. It's colder here in the deep shade of the oak tree.

I've seen the newspaper article about the traveler and heard the stories. I'm holding something that belonged to him—there's no question of that now. But a grave is an end. A period on the sentence. Who was he before this? How did he get here? He wasn't supposed to be in town for more than a night. Waiting a week for a delayed train turned into more than fifty years.

I close my fists slowly and take a deep breath.

I have to find out what happened. I've never felt so certain about anything. I plop down in the long grass and pull the packet of letters Mr. Sorensen gave me from my backpack. I thrust half of them to Syd.

Wordlessly she takes them and sits across from me. The three of us—me, Syd and the gravestone—could be a study group with a test on Monday.

The first thing I discover is that the *J* in *J.R.* stands for James. I glance at the gravestone. *Hi, James. Nice to meet you.*

As I read the first letter, I look for more clues to who he was. I'm half a page in when it hits me. I'm basically eavesdropping on a private conversation. The person who signed it, someone named Grace, seems to be J.R.'s older sister.

There isn't a lot in the letter to tell me about J.R., since it's a letter *to* him. I don't care about Grace's toddler or how her new job is going. If I were a historian, I might be interested in her opinions on the news. But I'm not. I want to know about J.R.

By the time I've gone through four letters, a fog of disappointment has crept over me. My eyes scan the letters, but I'm not really paying attention anymore. Then a sentence jumps out at me. I snap to attention and reread it.

I hope your trip goes well. You have some excited nieces eager to meet you. They're thrilled you're bringing them gifts from across the sea. I had to show them on the globe how far you're coming from. I can't believe it's been five years since I've seen you.

Gifts? How was that possible if the innkeeper found barely enough money to cover the room? Mr. Sorensen said his grandfather loved trinkets. Surely he'd have accepted items from Europe as payment if J.R. ran through his money on the trip home. If he didn't have any of them on him, where are they? The nagging question is back. How did he end up dead?

As the dark thoughts swirl around me, Syd's eyes widen at the letter she's reading. It's the last one.

"You need to see this," Syd says.

Still feeling glum, I begin to read. Instead of the *Dear James* I've gotten used to, this one begins with *Dear Grace*. I clutch the paper and read faster.

J.R. tells his sister how frustrated he is about the delayed train. It's his last connection before he gets home. While most of the townsfolk have been kind, he fears a few *unsavory* ones may try to rob him before the train arrives. He plans to hide his lockbox upriver that very evening. There's a rough sketch at the bottom of the page, and I recognize it straight away as my river. He finishes the letter with *I will post this in the morning. I hope I follow this letter by only a few days.*

I reread it twice. Syd stares at me with big eyes. When I finally look up, I know I must have the same look on my face. This is *huge*.

What happened to J.R. between writing this letter and being found dead at the inn? Did he hide his lockbox in time? Could his treasure still be out there, waiting to be found?

Chapter Eight

Thoughts of silver goblets and jeweled necklaces fill my mind. The image of me digging my fingers into a pile of gold coins is so vivid I can almost see the lockbox in front of me. J.R.'s treasure is out there. I just have to find it. Well, it *could* be out there, as long as he was able to hide it before the people he feared caught him.

Who in our town could have bothered him like that? Everyone's so nice—oh. Not *everyone*. Not the boys who taunt me from the safety of numbers. My excitement shrinks like a balloon losing air. I thought I wouldn't have to deal with bullies once I was older. No school, no bullies, right? But if they're always going to be there, then I can't keep running away. Just the thought of standing up to them makes my stomach clench.

I need a distraction.

Syd's half of the letters sits in her lap as she types on my phone. She never bothers to ask if she can borrow it. We have an understanding.

"Did you find anything?" I ask.

"Hm? Oh, not much. But I did find *this*." She shoves the phone at me.

There's already a comment on my photo of the grave. User Em_loves_raptors posted, *Does that say J. Reid? That was my grandma's brother's name! I think he died in the '60s too.*

I glance at Syd and can't help my frown. "It's just a coincidence."

"But what if it isn't?" Syd sizzles with excitement. She's usually so steady. It'd be funny how worked up she's getting if the situation weren't life and death.

"We'd need to verify her story—"

Syd reaches over and scrolls down. Without bothering to log out of *my* account, she replies to the comment with *What's your grandma's name?* I grumble at her for this abuse of privilege, but she's still scrolling. Em_loves_raptors replies, *Grace.*

Same name as the person who wrote these letters. I shake my head sharply. "Coincidence!"

"Maybe, but the lead is worth pursuing." Syd sits back with a smug smile. "I invited her to come out tomorrow. She doesn't live far from here."

Alarm spikes through my veins. "Syd! She could be an ax murderer!"

"Oh, please. Do you take me for an amateur? I've seen my pop run a million background checks. He's got to make sure he isn't buying stolen laptops. Em_loves_raptors, real name Emily, let us follow her private feed. It's legit. She's a few years older than us and lives up the road in Eagleside. Her granny is named Grace, just like James's sister! We'll meet her at my pop's shop or the café, with plenty of people around."

"Okay, probably not an ax murderer. But I don't have anything to show her except these letters and a pocket watch. I don't know what happened to J.R. *or* his lockbox. She's going to be disappointed."

"If she's actually related to this guy, she might have answers for *you*. Isn't that worth checking out?"

My shoulders sag as I sigh. Syd's right. A good detective follows all leads.

Syd's stomach gurgles so loud I can hear it from where I'm sitting. We lock eyes for a split second. Her short burst of laughter shatters the silence. "Almost dinnertime! I gotta get home. See you tomorrow!"

She hands me the other half of the letters and ruffles my hair as she stands to head out. I bat her hand away, and she laughs. My curls are wild enough as it is.

"See you," I say as I watch her leave. She lifts a hand in farewell without turning around.

The angle of the sunlight through the trees is a lot lower than when we arrived. Syd's loud stomach has reminded mine of how late it's gotten. I guess it's time to pack up. I tie the letters with their ribbon and put them in my backpack. The photocopies Ms. Vardanyan gave me are in there as well. I'd almost forgotten about them.

I'm not ready to leave J.R., so I flip through the photocopies. As I expected, they're mostly newspaper articles, but one page stands out. It's grainy and hard to read. The letterhead is from the town coroner's office. *Whoa.* My eyes jump straight to *Cause of death: misadventure.*

What does *that* mean? What's a misadventure, and how did it lead to J.R. dying in an armchair at the inn? The coroner must be protecting someone— like the people J.R. wanted to hide his lockbox from. I don't understand why, but bullies always seem to get away with being awful. No one ever wants to stand up to them, or they don't believe that "such nice boys" could do anything bad.

My lip quivers, and I'm frowning so hard my face starts to hurt. Sadness and anger fight each other inside me. I stare hard at the simple letters and numbers on the gravestone. J.R.'s lain here all this time, all alone, while the truth was hidden and almost lost.

This whole town is complicit in a cover-up. I decide right then and there to find J.R.'s lockbox and give it to his sister's granddaughter. He may not be able to finish his journey, but his gifts can.

I pack up my backpack, lay a hand on the gravestone and slowly walk away.

As I leave the shade of the trees and walk across the sports field next to the cemetery, I read the watch's inscription over and over. *We are with you always.* My thoughts are swirling so fast, they're hard to catch.

A shout behind me breaks through. Despite the warmth of the late afternoon, goose bumps prickle across my arms. A glance over my shoulder confirms my worst fear. Five boys on bikes are barreling toward me.

The buildings on the other side of the field are too far away. I'll never make it.

Chapter Nine

I start to run. Terror makes it hard to breathe. My panting sounds like a high-pitched wheeze. I'm squeezing the watch so tight the metal digs into my skin. My backpack flops wildly as I run faster than I've ever run before.

The big old oak tree in the middle of the field is my only hope. I can hear the boys getting closer. I swing my backpack off and fling it into the lower branches, praying to anything that'll listen that it stays up there. The pack starts to fall through the branches, and one of them catches a strap. It holds.

My backpack's safe, but it's too late for me. The boys circle their bikes. I'm trapped. My pounding heart is two seconds from exploding.

The boys have never done more than taunt me. When we were younger, they'd shove me on the playground. I'm not the only one they pick on, but I think I'm their favorite. Lucky me. They think it's funny how scared I get. They don't understand that conflict crumples everything inside me into a tinfoil ball. All sharp edges and impossible to smooth without tearing.

I wish I could stand up to them. I wish my hands weren't shaking so hard.

Brayden stands on his pedals as he rolls toward me, glaring hard. He hops off his bike and lets it fall to the grass. The others are sneering and laughing. I don't dare look at them. Brayden walks right up to me. He's a good two inches shorter, but it doesn't matter. He makes up for it with bile and spite. He's so close, I can see a bruise fading under one of his eyes.

"Thanks for telling us exactly where you were, nerd. Saved us a lot of hunting."

Confused, I risk a glance at the others. One of them waves a phone displaying my photo of the grave. My stomach drops as I put it together. Brayden is the one who left the threat on my first photo of the watch. They've been following me around all day.

"Why do you want me to give the watch back? To who?"

"Some secrets need to be protected," Brayden says.

Despite the bad situation I'm in, curiosity makes me speak. "What kind of secrets? Secrets like who took J.R. back to the inn the night he died?" It's a wild guess, but I have to take it. That line from the article at the museum has been bothering me. Mr. Sorensen's mother found his body, but who were the two men who were the last to see him alive?

Brayden's eyes go wide. My hunch was right! He knows!

"Shut up!" Brayden snatches the watch from my hand. In an instant my fear comes crashing back, and I'm too frozen to fight him.

Everything is frozen for a moment. Brayden and I stare at each other, his flash of anger gone as what he did sinks in. He's scared too—though not as scared as I am. It's *his* friends who surround us.

If I do nothing, I'll never see the watch again. I try to form words, but my throat is tight. I can't even move. Brayden looks like he's going to be sick, but he shoves it down with a grimace.

"Come on!" He grabs his bike and speeds away. The other boys glance at each other, shrug and follow him.

I'm left alone in the middle of the field. My hand is still held in front of me, fingers curled around nothing. With the watch gone, I have nothing.

A breeze ripples across the field. The branches of the oak tree creak. I almost forgot about my backpack.

Usually I love climbing trees, but this time it's a struggle. The bark scrapes my fingers as I pull myself up. Twigs and leaves rain down and bounce off my face. It feels like forever before I get to the branch with my backpack. I pull it free and jump the ten or so feet to the ground. I land with a grunt and roll. I know I'm covered in bits of grass, but I don't care.

I've let J.R. down. He was trying to protect his treasures from those thieves, and now the grandson of one of them has his prized watch. All because of me. Because I can't stand up to people when things get intense.

I did get one thing out of the showdown though. I've confirmed that foul play was involved. There was no mysterious illness or bad health. My guess is Brayden's grandfather and his friend roughed up J.R. to find out where the treasure was hidden. But I don't think he told them.

What does knowing that matter now? The truth won't change what happened or bring J.R. back.

The field feels a million times wider than it should. My head hangs low, and my sneakers crunch dying grass, one slow step at a time.

Emily is coming tomorrow, expecting a pocket watch and answers.

I don't have either for her.

Chapter Ten

I can't sleep.

My phone says it's 4:02 a.m.

The letters and papers I've collected are spread over my bed. I've read them all twice. I know the names of J.R.'s parents, his siblings and his sister's children. All things Emily already knows.

From what I can tell, J.R. decided to go traveling in his early twenties. Except for the letter he didn't get to send, all I have are the replies to him, but Grace has helped me fill in the blanks with clues in her letters. He was gone for a long time, and he saw a lot of bad and a lot of good. He missed his family and decided to go home.

Without the details, it isn't a very exciting story. I wish I could read the letters J.R. wrote or talk to him somehow. I'd ask him how it was so easy for him to take off into the unknown. Did he feel lost in his hometown too?

When I'd held his watch, anything had felt possible. I'd thought, *Maybe when I'm older I can travel too. I can leave Cedarbrook and see the world. The town will still be here to come home to. The river will still run, and the bridge isn't going anywhere. I just have to be brave.*

With the watch gone, snatched right out of my hand, I'm less sure.

I want the river to be enough, like it used to be. I want my town to be enough.

And I don't want to worry about bullies around every corner.

The light on my silenced phone flashes. Another comment. Ever since I posted the photo of the watch, the likes and comments have been piling up. I haven't posted anything since the grave. My followers are getting hungry for updates. What can I tell them? That I was too scared to defend a piece of local history? But if I *had* stood up to Brayden, who knows what he—and his friends—would have done to me.

In the deep dark of night, only one thing feels right. I sift through the letters until I find what I'm looking for. With my bedside lamp at an angle, I take a photo of the last lines of the letter.

Come home soon.

Love,

Grace

I sit back to admire the framing. It looks almost professional.

The caption is harder. I tap the back of my phone while I go over a hundred different lines. None of them sound right in my head. Whatever I post, I know Brayden will see it too.

I swipe over to my conversation with Syd to read it for the fiftieth time. I messaged her after dinner to tell her what happened.

Don't worry, Theo. We'll get it back.

How?

We'll think of something. Brayden's a jerk, but not that tough.

Easy for you to say.

If you do my superhero bootcamp, you'll be standing up to the Forces of Evil in no time.

Yeah, like that will ever happen.

Don't give up! Bridge after lunch. Bring your gear.

I take a deep breath. Tomorrow. It's all happening tomorrow.

Back at my in-progress post, I type in a caption.

I read it over. I say it under my breath so I can hear the words.

"I'm not giving up."

No one knows the river better than me. If anyone's going to find J.R.'s lost treasure and give it to his family, it's me. I can't let him down.

He's been waiting too long.

Chapter Eleven

I beat Syd to the bridge, which gives me a moment to breathe. The river tumbles below my feet, whispering its secrets. Folks walk along the paths parallel to the river, biking, jogging, walking dogs. Their laughter and conversations flow with the water sounds.

Feet crunch on gravel behind me. I brace for the worst, but it's just Syd. The backpack slung over her shoulder has strange bulges in it. *Uh-oh*. When Syd decides she cares about something, she goes all in. I grin as she hurries up to me, a little out of breath. I'm glad I'm not the only one who wants to help J.R.

"What'd you bring?" I ask.

"So much stuff! I have to take it back to the shop in good condition, so be careful with it." She slings off her backpack, and it lands on the wooden boards with a clunk. When she unzips it, there's all sorts of jumbled things inside, but the first thing she pulls out is—

"A metal detector!" It isn't a full-length one like people use in fields and beaches to find lost wrecks and tombs and stuff. This is more of a wide baton. I can wave it through the air or stick it in bushes and it'll tell me if there's any metal close by.

"Thought it would help." She holds it out to me like it's a royal sword.

I take it with the gravity it deserves. "This is perfect."

Syd rummages through her backpack and shows me the rest. None of it will be as useful as the metal detector. I just want to get to the water and start looking.

"This at least?" Syd toggles a headlamp on and off.

"Syd." I point at the afternoon sun.

She rolls her eyes and shoves the headlamp into her backpack. "What if there's a cave?"

I take out the letter J.R. never sent. I'm sure the river has changed over the last fifty years. Not *too* much, I hope. The sketch of the river is rough, but it has the bend and the big rock. I can use those to find my way. I just hope the lockbox is still in the same place as the X on the map.

Syd gives me a walkie-talkie, and I give her the map.

She tries to push other things on me, like rope and elbow pads. I'm certain she has a grappling-hook gun in there. The only thing I take is a pair of thick yellow gloves. Syd doesn't hide her disappointment.

"What was the point of bringing all this if you aren't going to use it?" she demands.

"I'll help you carry it back," I say over my shoulder as I head for the slope down to the river.

Loose stones roll under my waterproof shoes. The momentum sends me sliding wildly the rest of the way. I hit the water with a splash. It's shallower on this side because of the current. But even at only six inches deep, the water pulls and tugs at my ankles.

As I reach the bend in the river, the big rock comes into clearer view. I shade my eyes to look back at Syd. It's hard to see her with the afternoon sun creeping down behind her.

My walkie-talkie crackles to life and Syd says, "You're close! Just a little farther."

She's sitting on the planks with her legs dangling over the side, and she's clutching the walkie-talkie. I forgot she gets nervous on the bridge—but it's the middle of the day. No self-respecting ghosts come out in the day.

I throw her a thumbs-up before pushing onward, out of her sight. It's just me and J.R. now.

The metal detector makes an electronic chirp when I turn it on. I wave it over the bushes growing along the bank. The rocks are slippery, so I have to go slow.

The lockbox is close—I can feel it.

On another swing with no sound from the detector, I check my position against the big rock again. That's when I see him. Brayden. He's sitting on a bench on the opposite bank, his head in his hands. I freeze. I could jump in the bushes to hide—I shake my head at myself. There's a whole river between us. He can't get me here.

Brayden must sense me watching him, because he looks up. We stare at each other for a long, terrible moment. Then he jumps on his bike and rides away.

I breathe a sigh of relief—until I remember the bridge is downriver. Syd! I take two steps before I remember no one messes with her. She's too tough and never backs down.

I'll worry about what Brayden's up to later. Right now the important thing is finding J.R.'s treasure.

A few feet farther on, the metal detector makes a faint chirp. I freeze. I pass the detector back over the bushes. Another chirp.

Okay. *Okay*. This could just as easily be a pile of old cans as a treasure lost for decades.

I pull the branches out of the way with one hand while the other brandishes the detector like a sword. I zero in on some dense plants. The chirping is going crazy now. I stow the detector in my waistband and use both hands to clear away the plants and dirt. My gloved fingers skim over cold metal. *Flat* metal. Not cans.

Under a layer of dirt and debris, the lockbox waits. It's really here.

As I reach for it, I feel like I'm reaching through time. J.R. outsmarted the people trying to rob him. His treasures are safe.

I grip the edges and pull. It's stuck tight. With a lot of shifting, rocking and grunting, I finally manage to wobble it. I brace my feet and *pull*. The lockbox comes loose, and I stumble back into the water with a splash.

The lockbox is heavier than I expected. I hug it to my chest and take careful steps toward the bridge. I can hear things shifting inside. What could be in there? It doesn't sound like coins or jeweled crowns.

As I round the bend, Syd jumps to her feet. My walkie-talkie crackles to life.

"*It's real!*" The excitement in her voice makes me grin.

Seeing Syd reminds me of the other person lurking near the river. My smile slips. I adjust the lockbox against my hip so I can reach my walkie-talkie. "Have you seen anyone while I was gone?"

"No one specific. Just the usual joggers and walkers. Are you expecting someone?"

Not expecting, dreading. Her answer doesn't put me at ease. Brayden could be watching the bridge from a hiding place, waiting for me. I tighten my grip on the lockbox. I'm not going to let fear ruin this for me.

With every step down the river, the water rushes past my ankles, hurrying me along. I stagger up the bank and Syd meets me halfway, helping me the rest of the way to the top. Together we set the lockbox down in a cleared area beside a bench.

We sit to catch our breath, grinning like loons at the lost treasure between us. I've swum past the spot where it lay a million times, never knowing it was there.

Syd leans forward. "Well? What are you waiting for?"

Chapter Twelve

The metal box is in terrible condition. The lock isn't huge, but it's rusted and stiff. When I tug on it, flakes of rust and moss come off in my hand. Just as I'm thinking of trying to stomp it open like in the movies, Syd nudges me aside.

"Is that a screwdriver?"

"Trust me." She slides the screwdriver through the loop of the lock, pushes down and...nothing.

She growls and puts her full weight behind it. *Crunch.* The lock breaks and hangs open.

"Whoa. Nice," I say.

We each hold a corner of the lid and lift together.

I imagine a silver saber in a jeweled scabbard. Or a gold pen engraved with the name of a king. Anything I can show off on my feed. Something to prove my river is still worth exploring and my town is worth staying in.

Just as my heart is lifting in hope…it plummets to the ground and shatters. All that's inside are wads of newspaper gone brown with age.

"What? No!" I fall back in utter disappointment. I needed this to be good.

"Don't be dramatic." Syd gingerly takes one of the wads of newspaper and unfolds it. "There, see?" A small train engine made of tin sits in her palm. "They're wrapped for protection."

"Oh." I guess a tin train engine is all right, even if it isn't a gold pen. Anything's better than a handful of fishing lures. Someone's missing this, even if they don't know it yet, and I can return it to them.

As I reach for one of the wads, I pause and tilt my head. I've had this nagging feeling I should be paying attention. Just then I notice the sound—someone's crossing the bridge, but they're slowing as they get close to us.

An intense need to protect this box comes over me. J.R. protected it for over fifty years. Now it's my turn. I spring to my feet and face the person, already knowing who I'm going to see.

Brayden stops fifteen feet away.

My fists are shaking by my sides, but I'm not going to freeze this time. If I'm the boulder in the river, he can't push me around.

"You can't have this. Back off." I have no idea where the words come from. Maybe it's J.R. standing with me.

Instead of answering, Brayden looks away.

There's something different about him today. His shoulders are hunched, and his frown is stubborn instead of mad. His bike leans at a sad angle. He reaches into his pocket and, without looking at me, shoves the watch toward me. "Here."

I'm too shocked to move. Brayden takes a step forward. "Take it!" When I cringe away from him, he gets the same surprised expression he did when he first took the watch. Like he doesn't know he's scary. His face flushes red. "I don't want to protect an angry old man anymore. My grandpa doesn't deserve it. I don't want to be like him. Please, take it back."

One of the last pieces fits into place. Brayden knew about the watch's history because his grandfather was one of the young men who tried to rob J.R. The shadow of a bruise still darkens Brayden's eye. No wonder he's so mean. He hasn't known anything different.

Our hands brush when I take the watch from him. He flinches a little.

"Thanks," I say.

Brayden frowns fiercely. He mutters, "Don't thank me."

"Do you...do you know what happened to him?" The words are hard to say. I'm not sure I want to know, even after all this time spent chasing the truth.

"I've pieced it together," Brayden says slowly. "My grandpa says stuff when he drinks. He and his buddy were trying to rough up a guy they thought was a rich out-of-towner. But they pushed him too hard, and he hit his head." Brayden jerks his chin toward one of the metal supports on the bridge. "On one of those. They thought he'd be okay if they took him back to the inn. But, well, you know. He wasn't."

The world sways around me as Brayden's words sink in. *Oh man.* I press a hand against one of the supports, feeling the sun-warmed metal on my skin. Something catches my eye behind Brayden. A girl at the other end of the bridge watches us.

Brayden follows my gaze. "Who's that?"

She's pretty far away, and I've only seen her in photos, but there's no mistaking who she is. "She came for J.R."

Brayden's eyes widen, like he was just caught next to a graffitied wall with a spray can in his hand. "I gotta go." He throws a leg over his bike, but before he takes off, he says, "This doesn't make us friends or anything, but...I'm sorry, okay? Jeez."

I watch him go, too stunned to speak. Did Brayden Boone just *apologize* to me? Does this mean he's going to stop picking on me? For a wild moment I imagine Brayden and the other bullies sitting in a circle, talking about their feelings.

Yeah. No. I'm not holding my breath for that.

Before meeting Emily, aka Em_loves_raptors, I run my thumb over the ship engraved on the watch lid. I worried about what Brayden might do to the watch while he had it, but it's no different than it was yesterday. The hinge protests, but it opens for me to read the inscription. *Sail fearlessly.*

I take a deep breath. This is it. Emily's walking straight for me, and for some reason I'm nervous. I hope she likes what I've found. I hurry to meet her partway down the bridge.

She smiles and waves. "You must be Theo."

"Um. Yeah." Emily's brown hair is braided and flung over her shoulder. Freckles are dashed over her nose, under big blue eyes. How similar does she look to J.R.? It's not like there's a good description of the ghost. Who isn't real. "I thought we were going to meet at the café?"

Emily chuckles, a little embarrassed. "Sorry, I got here early and figured I'd see the place where—" She bites her lip. "Is this...?"

Now *I'm* embarrassed. My dumb town made up a story about a real person who left behind a real family. "Sort of. The story around here is that your great-uncle haunts this bridge." As soon as the words leave my mouth, I'm mortified. Was that insensitive? "*I've* never seen him." As if that would be consolation! I'm mentally punching myself, but Emily looks pensive.

"Huh. That's pretty cool. Not many people can say they're related to a ghost."

"Um. No, I guess not." I'm not sure what to say. Usually it's *Hey, I found your phone. Okay, bye.* They're surprised, delighted, and sometimes they hug me. It's pretty great. This is in a whole other league. May as well stick with what I know. "Since you're here, want to see what we found?"

Emily's eyes light up. "I do! And I'll show you what I brought."

Chapter Thirteen

Syd, Emily and I sit on the ground around the open box. Emily takes out a long item, but before she unwraps it, she peers at the newspaper.

"This is from January 1967...from Paris!"

"Really?" I smooth the paper the tin train was wrapped in. Sure enough, even my so-so French lets me decipher the headlines and some of the text. I know J.R. traveled, that he came from afar, but holding this proof all the way from Europe makes it so much more real. And I almost didn't notice. I need to work on my detective skills.

Emily pulls apart the newspaper, careful not to rip it. Inside is a wooden dog on wheels, with a braided leash.

"Who was that for?" Syd asks.

"Maybe my dad? Oh, wait…1967…he wasn't born until three years later! *Weird.*"

"What about Helen, your aunt?" I ask.

Emily stares at me like *I'm* an ax murderer. "How do you know about Aunt Helen?"

"Um. We…" The way she's looking at me makes my insides curdle. I'm not a snoop!

Syd rescues me. "She was mentioned in your grandma's letters. We'll show you in a second."

"Oh, cool. I forgot about those."

Next we unwrap a teacup with a matching saucer for Emily's great-aunt. Then there's a wooden pipe for Emily's grandpa, who passed away five years ago. The last one is a silver brooch in the shape of a bird.

"That must be for Granny," Emily says. "I wonder what she'll think of it."

I feel a spark of hope. It's not too late. Grace will get her gift.

They're all perfectly normal things, and yet they're treasures. They were all chosen with some-one in mind, and most of them will be able to find their way to who they were meant for.

None of these cost as much as a phone, but I'm brimming with so much happiness, I can hardly speak. It's always great to see someone's excitement and relief when I return their lost things. Though it isn't why I keep coming back to the river, it's a perk. *This*, though. This is bigger. More important. There was a hole in Emily's family story, and I've filled it in. It's like someone flipped a light switch inside me and I'm glowing from the inside out.

"Your grandma will want these too." I dig into my backpack for the packet of letters. They're still tied with the ribbon.

"Oh *wow*." Emily holds the letters gently, like they're about to fall apart in her hands. "That's her handwriting, all right." Emily slips the packet into her satchel and takes out a big yellow envelope. "I brought some things to show you too."

I close the lid of the lockbox to turn it into a small table. Emily spreads out some old, faded photos. Syd and I lean in to see, so close our shoulders press together.

The first photo shows a guy who's between his late teens and early twenties, standing in front of a house. I can see the family resemblance in Emily—same wavy, light-brown hair, same smile. He's wearing a casual suit and grinning, one hand in his pocket and the other one holding—the watch! I suck in a breath and hold it, as if I'm about to go down for a deep dive.

"That's James after his second year of college. He decided to take a break before finishing, so he could travel. One year turned into five. My grandma doesn't talk about her brother very much, but it sounds like he fell in love with discovery. New people, new places—he wanted to find them all."

"Wait, she doesn't talk about him?" Syd looks horrified by this.

"It makes her too sad, I think," Emily says. "They were really close. She named my dad after him."

"Wouldn't it be better to remember the good times? Keep his memory alive with stories?"

Emily shrugs. "I couldn't tell you. I don't think she ever figured out how to get there."

The other photos look like they came straight out of a family album. James in a holiday sweater next to a Christmas tree. James and his siblings at a lake. I recognize the mountains behind them—my mom took me there last summer. There are even a couple of photos he must have sent with his letters.

He's posing next to the Eiffel Tower in one and at Stonehenge in another.

He looks like a regular guy. And for the last fifty or so years, my town's been convinced he's haunting our bridge. But he just wanted to get back home to see his family.

Emily gathers the photos to put them away. "Thanks for finding my great-uncle. He was missing for a long time. Back in 1967, Granny waited all day at the train station for him. Even after the train he was supposed to be on came and went." After a second she meets my eyes. Hers are bright, and so's her smile. "You should come meet my granny sometime. You know how to reach me."

"Wait. Before you go, there's one more thing." My fingers curl around the watch in my pocket for the last time. "Here." My outstretched hand is trembling, but I don't know how to make it stop.

Emily shakes her head, still smiling. "Keep it. Great-Uncle James would want you to have it."

Did she just say what I think she said? "Really?"

Syd elbows me in the ribs and says to Emily, "He *means* thank you."

"Y-yeah, thanks." I cradle the watch close to my chest. I'm not sure what to feel. All sorts of things are swirling around, and I can't quite catch any of them. I run my thumb over the inscription. *Sail fearlessly.*

That message is for me now.

Syd stands when Emily does. "Want to see the town? I can show you the inn where J.R. stayed. It's a bookstore now."

"Sure, that'd be cool."

Syd hefts the lockbox into her arms. "You coming, Theo?"

"You go ahead. I'll catch up."

My throat is tight as I watch Syd and Emily cross the bridge. Their voices fade until there's nothing but the rush of the river.

I push myself to my feet and wander to the center of the bridge. There's a calm inside me I'm not used to. Like a boulder in the river, sitting quietly while the world hurries by. Boulders don't care what gets shouted at them. It doesn't change who they are.

I don't know what's coming tomorrow, but I know I can ride the current.

The sun is setting orange and brilliant. My shadow stretches far behind me, onto the tumbling water below. I solved a mystery, and I helped a traveler finish his journey. I forgot to take photos of the treasures we found, but that's okay. That's not why I dive in the river.

The sun sinks behind the mountains. Over the sound of the river, I hear a train whistle in the distance.

NOW WHAT?

CHECK OUT MORE GREAT READS IN THE

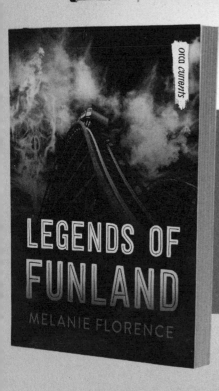

Buddy and his friends are determined to prove their bravery by spending the night at a haunted amusement park.

READ ON FOR A SNEAK PEEK!

Where are you?

The text was from Ryan. Buddy stuffed the phone back into his pocket without responding. Let him wonder where he was. He hoped Ryan was worried. But then he remembered he had told his mom he was staying at Jimmy's. Ryan would just ask her where he was. In any case, he really didn't think he owed his brother a response. Ryan hadn't apologized for yelling at him or saying he was always in the way. He'd be sorry tomorrow when everyone was talking about how Buddy had spent the night at Funland. He'd be a legend, and his brother would be begging to hang out with him.

"Hey! Earth to Buddy!" Steph waved her hand in front of Buddy's face. "What do you want to do first?"

"Sorry. Umm…I guess the bumper cars?"

"Yes!" Jimmy punched the air. "You are going down! I'm so good at bumper cars. Seriously. I should go pro."

"Last time, you ran into the wall and couldn't get back into the middle," Steph reminded him. "You literally were wedged against the wall the entire time. You didn't hit a single person."

"Yeah. But the times before that, I was great."

"I think you even cried a little," she said, laughing.

"I did *not* cry!" Jimmy was laughing too.

"I think you did," she teased. "I definitely saw a tear or two."

"No way! Bumper-car pros do not cry."

"I bet I can make you cry this time." She grinned.

"You're going down!" Jimmy repeated. "Soooo down, Steph!"

Buddy watched as his friends jostled each other and laughed. He wanted to join in. But all he could think about was the look on his brother's face when he found out they had spent the night at the park.

I'll show him, he thought.

The rest of the evening passed in a whirlwind of food, rides and games. Jimmy was not having much luck winning anything.

"I think these games are rigged," he told them as they walked away from the ring-toss booth.

"You're just realizing that?" Steph asked. "They are *definitely* rigged. The rings are made to bounce off the pegs. And the basket toss is just as bad."

"What do you mean?" Jimmy asked.

"They have the baskets tipped just enough to bounce the ball back out every single time," Buddy told him. "Everyone knows that. It's physics."

"No it's not." Steph rolled her eyes. "It's geometry. Jimmy! Seriously? You can't be hungry again!"

Jimmy had stopped in front of the chip truck. "We have to hide soon. I don't want to be hungry."

"Shh!" Buddy pulled him close. "Not so loud. Someone will hear."

"Dude. We're by the Death Drop. *That's* all anyone can hear."

"Yeah, I guess you're right. I'm just nervous." Buddy looked at his watch. The park would be closing in less than an hour.

"Okay. We have about a half hour until we have to hide." He whispered the last few words, glancing around to make sure no one overheard them. "Does anyone need to pee?" As soon as he said it, he regretted it. He was not their mom! But Jimmy and Steph both raised their hands. "Okay. Let's take care of that first and then we can grab one last snack. Once we're back in the kids' section, you can get started on the security system, Steph."

Within minutes they were walking back through the park, stuffing fries into their mouths.

"I really hope I don't get hungry later," Jimmy

said between mouthfuls. "I should have got something extra just in case."

"Don't worry. I brought granola bars," Steph told him.

There was a chain blocking the entrance to the kiddie section, but after a quick scan of the area, the three friends climbed over and walked quickly down the path.

"Wait!" Buddy called out, pulling them to the side and off the walkway. "Look." He pointed at a video camera aimed down on the path.

"We should have done this sooner. Give me a minute," Steph said. They walked a little deeper into the trees lining the path so they were hidden. With any luck, they hadn't been picked up on any of the cameras before they'd had a chance to disable them.

Steph sat down and pulled out her laptop. By the time Buddy and Jimmy settled in beside her, she was tapping furiously on her keyboard.

"Can you find the cameras?" Buddy asked.

"Shh. Give me a minute."

Buddy and Jimmy moved a bit farther away to give her space to work.

"So…do you think the park is really haunted?" Jimmy asked.

"Nah," Buddy said, shaking his head. "There's no such thing as ghosts. It's just a story some kid started, and it got repeated over and over until it became a spooky legend."

"I don't know. My uncle said he saw the ghost once," Jimmy said. "He was riding the Death Drop and looked down, and it was standing in the entrance to the haunted house."

"He saw a ghost standing in the entrance to the haunted house?"

"Yeah. That's what he says."

"How can he be sure it wasn't just a staff member *dressed* as a ghost? One of the ones working the haunted house?" Buddy asked.

"I don't know. He just said it looked like a ghost."

"Well, yeah. That's kind of the point of the haunted house."

"Got it!" Steph said, lifting her arms in triumph. "Now I will just set it to run video from yesterday…riiiiight….NOW!" She hit a key and studied her screen for a few more seconds. "Yes! It worked. It's running a second-by-second replay from yesterday that matches the current time. If they do their rounds at the same time every night, they won't even notice."

"But isn't the date marked on it?" Buddy asked.

"Nope. Just the time. The date is buried in the metadata. They'd have no reason to check that. It's older software. If they upgrade it, it will have the date stamp. But we got lucky."

"Could you have fixed it if it *did* have a full time stamp?" Buddy asked.

"Of course!" Steph grinned.

"You're amazing," Buddy said, coming over to give her a high five. And then Jimmy got into the act and high-fived them both. "So I guess we can get into position now. It will take some time for the park to empty." Buddy led the way back to the path, looking both ways to make sure no one was around.

"All clear," Jimmy announced.

They didn't come across anyone on their way to the kiddie rides. The carousel was deserted. With no one around, it felt kind of creepy, Buddy had to admit. He wondered what the rest of the park would be like. He walked around the carousel until he found the door to the base. It was closed with a simple latch, which he opened. He pulled a flashlight out of his bag and shone it around underneath.

"Empty," he called back over his shoulder.

"No spiders?" Jimmy asked. He hated spiders.

"I don't see any. Looks pretty clean. No webs."

"Snakes?" Steph asked, shuddering. "There better not be any snakes."

"Nope. Nothing." Buddy crawled in and then moved aside to let his friends squeeze in too. He pulled the door shut behind them.

"Now all we have to do is wait."

Allison Finley has a BFA in creative writing from the University of British Columbia. She works as a freelance writer and editor. Allison gratefully lives next to a river just outside of Vancouver, British Columbia, on the ancestral, traditional and unceded territory of the Kwikwetlem First Nation.

For more information on all the books

in the Orca Currents line, please visit

orcabook.com